To Sally

Text and illustrations copyright © 1980 by Jenny Partridge
Published by World's Work Ltd
The Windmill Press, Kingswood, Tadworth, Surrey
Layout and design by The Romany Studio Workshop
Reproduced by Graphic Affairs Ltd, Southend
Printed in Great Britain by
William Clowes (Beccles) Limited, Beccles and London
SBN 437 66170 9

Mr Squint

JENNY PARTRIDGE

A WORLD'S WORK CHILDREN'S BOOK

"Hmm, now let me see," said the old mole, scratching his head. He searched under his cobbler's bench and brought out a roll of rosy red leather, but the little field vole shook her head sadly.

"It's very nice, I'm sure," said her
grandmother, old Mrs Twitcher,
"but I'm afraid young Verity has set
her heart on purple shoes!"
"Dear me," said Mr Squint.
"I haven't anything that colour!"

A tear rolled down Verity's face and
splashed on his workbench.

"Oh, please, Mr Squint, I must have
some shoes by Friday, to wear to the
party at Mayfly Manor!"

When he saw how unhappy she was,
he winked.

"Well, I shall have to see what I can do.

Come back on Friday morning and you
will have your purple shoes."
Verity clapped her paws in excitement.
"Thank you," said Mrs Twitcher.
"What a kind mole you are!"
Mr Squint blushed, and adjusted his
glasses. Happy now, they said goodbye,
and left the shop.

"Dear me," muttered Mr Squint, "whatever shall I do? I simply can not disappoint young Verity, but where, oh where shall I find purple leather?"

He shook his head as he cleared his workbench and, humming to himself, he swept the little shop and locked up. Putting the key safely in his pocket, he began the walk home. It was a golden autumn evening in Oakapple Wood.

The trees and bushes hung heavy with blackberries, elderberries and rosehips. Deep in thought, the mole paused to rest under an elder tree.

"'Evening, Squint old fellow," said a
voice. It was Hopfellow. "What a
lovely evening for a spot of fishing!"
"Hmm, indeed," agreed Squint,
vaguely. They exchanged a few more
words of woodland gossip and then
with a wave the frog went on his way.

Squint turned to go, but suddenly his foot caught under a tree root and he clutched at a branch of elderberries to steady himself.

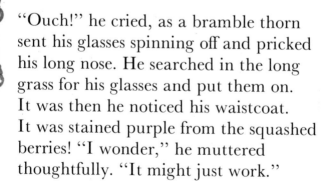

"Ouch!" he cried, as a bramble thorn
sent his glasses spinning off and pricked
his long nose. He searched in the long
grass for his glasses and put them on.
It was then he noticed his waistcoat.
It was stained purple from the squashed
berries! "I wonder," he muttered
thoughtfully. "It might just work."

He picked another branch and carefully carried the cluster of fruit home. Once inside his little house, the mole made himself a mug of blackberry leaf tea, and set to work.

He boiled the elderberries in water,
stirring them until the mixture became
a deep purple.

He strained it into a china bowl,
and carefully selected a piece of leather
so fine it felt like satin!
Laying it gently in the bowl, he watched
its colour slowly change.

He was quite unaware that, as he leant over the bowl, his neckerchief had

dipped into the dye and was now
half yellow and half purple!

He hung the leather out to dry and then
went wearily to bed.

Early next morning he found to his
delight that the leather had dried
to a lovely shade of purple.
After a breakfast of tea and oat-grass
scones, he hurried to his little shop,
the roll of leather under his arm.

All day long and late into the night, he
worked on the shoes, cutting the leather
and sewing the pieces together.
Who would have thought that those
great paws could have sewn such
tiny stitches?

Friday morning came at last, and a very
tired Mr Squint stood smiling at his two
early customers.

"Ooh, they're beautiful!" cried Verity,
dancing about in the purple shoes.
"Thank you, thank you, Mr Squint!"

"However did you manage in time?"
asked Mrs Twitcher. "And just the right
shade of purple too!"
The old mole beamed, and rubbed his
paws on his apron.

"Come along Verity," said her grandmother, "or we shall be late for the party. Goodbye Mr Squint, and thank you kindly once again!"

At the door, Verity stopped
and looked back, puzzled.

"Please, Mr Squint," she said.
"Why is your neckerchief half yellow
and half purple?"

Squint looked down, and suddenly
started to chuckle. "Well now, Verity,"

he said, winking at her,
"that's quite another story!"